FIRE RESCUE

EMERGENCY VEHICLES

Deborah Chancellor

Smart Apple Media

Published by Smart Apple Media,
an imprint of Black Rabbit Books
P.O. Box 3263, Mankato, Minnesota 56002
www.blackrabbitbooks.com

Published by arrangement with the Watts Publishing
Group LTD, London.

Library of Congress Cataloging-in-Publication Data
Chancellor, Deborah.
  Fire rescue / by Deborah Chancellor.
     pages cm. — (Emergency vehicles)
  Includes bibliographical references and index.
  Summary: "Introduces readers to eight different fire-
fighting vehicles, such as fire engines, planes, and boats.
Explains and diagrams how each is equipped to fight fires
in different locations. Includes a reading quiz and web
sites"—Provided by publisher.
  ISBN 978-1-59920-889-3 (library binding : alk. paper)
 1. Fire engines—Juvenile literature. 2. Fireboats—
Juvenile literature. 3. Emergency vehicles—Juvenile
literature. I. Title.
  TH9372.C43 2013
  628.9'259--dc23

Printed in the United States and Corporate Graphics,
North Mankato, Minnesota.

PO1634
11-2013

9 8 7 6 5 4 3 2

Series editor: Adrian Cole/Amy Stephenson
Editor: Sarah Ridley
Art direction: Peter Scoulding
Designer: Steve Prosser
Picture researcher: Diana Morris

Picture credits:
Sorin Alb/Shutterstock: 20-21.
Garry Blakeley/Shutterstock: 13.
Mike Brake/Shutterstock: 7.
Peter Byrne/PA Archive/PAI: 9.
daseaford/Shutterstock: 4.
Le Do/Shutterstock: 5.
www.firefighternation.com: 10-11.
Gertjan Hooljer/Shutterstock: 18.
Kecko/flickr: 16-17.
Kirsanov/Shutterstock: 11t.
Shay Levy/Photostock Israel/Alamy: 21t.
Pavel Losevsky/Shutterstock: 6.
Ian Nellist/Alamy: 8.
Ongchangwei/Dreamstime: 19.
ryasick/istockphoto: front cover.
Graeme Shannon/Shutterstock: 15.
Olaf Speler/Shutterstock: 14.
Stockfolio/Alamy: 12.

Every attempt has been made to clear copyright.
Should there be any inadvertent omission,
please apply to the publisher for rectification.

WHOOSH!

Contents

Sound and Light

A fire engine is coming! The noisy **siren** tells drivers to move out of the way.

HONK! HONK! HONK!

The engine carries special tools and **equipment**.

WHOOOOO! WHOOOOO!

Lights

Siren

Bell

Sky High

The long ladder on this engine stretches up and up to save people from fires in tall buildings.

CRANK! CRANK! WHIRRR! WHIRRR!

Firefighters climb the ladder to get close to the fire. They use a hose to blast water at the blaze.

The ladder is strong and safe.

Water

City Speed

Shiny fire motorcycles can roar through crowded streets and speed past traffic to the scene of a fire.

Big **panniers** carry fire fighting equipment and a first-aid kit.

FIRE

FIRE

RE54 MSO

The tank carries foam and water to put out small fires.

Off-road

This off-road fire truck reaches **wildfires** in far off places. It has a four-wheel drive and tough tires to help it move over bumpy ground.

BUMP!

Inside the cab, a **global positioning system (GPS)** helps the crew find the fire.

The fire truck carries a tank of water to put out leaping flames.

BUMP!

Air Attack

A fire plane attacks big wildfires from the air. It carries a tank and spraying equipment.

The plane scoops up water to fill its tanks.

WHOOSH!

WHOOSH!

The plane dumps water on the fire below.

13

Up and Away

This fire helicopter is on its way to an emergency. It dips a special bucket into the lake to fill it up with water.

CHUPPA!

WHUPPA!

WHUPPA!

CHUPPA!

WHOOSHH!

The noisy fire helicopter hovers above the fire, dropping water on the flames.

15

Fire Express

In some countries, special trains fight fires on railways, in tunnels, and near the track.

Water tank

PSSHHH!
PSSHHH!

Fire hose

A strong **locomotive** pulls heavy tanks, pumps, and **power generators** to the scene of the fire.

PSSHHH!
PSSHHH!

Pump and Spray

The fireboat has rushed to a burning ship. It pumps water from under the fireboat and aims it at the flames.

SPLASH!

WHOOSH!

A fireboat tests out its water jets in Hong Kong harbor.

Water jets shoot out of **nozzles**.

WHOOOSHH!

WHOOSH!

Crash Site

An **airport fire vehicle** smashes through barriers to reach a burning plane on the runway.

WHOOSHHH!

FFSOOT

Powerful pumps spray foam and water at the fire.

A mechanical arm lifts a hose above the flames.

SPLASH!

EMERGENCY SERVICES

16

Glossary

airport fire vechile
a fire engine that is specially
designed to fight airport fires

equipment
the items you need to
do something

**global positioning
system (GPS)**
a piece of equipment that uses
information received from a
satellite to give directions

locomotive
the engine that pulls a train

nozzle
the spout at the end of a hose

panniers
boxes and bags on
the back of a bike

power generator
machinery that makes electricity

siren
a loud hooting or wailing sound

two-way radio
a radio set you use to
talk to somebody far away

wildfire
a fire that destroys forests and
other plant life

Quiz

1. Why do fire motorcycles have flashing lights?

2. Why do fire engines carry ladders?

3. Why do fire engines need sirens?

4. How do fire helicopters collect water?

5. What are fire trains for?

6. What is an airport fire vehicle?

Answers:

1. Flashing lights make fire motorcycles easy to see in traffic.

2. Ladders help firefighters reach tall buildings.

3. A fire engine's sirens warn vehicles to slow down and move out of the way.

4. Fire helicopters use buckets to scoop up water.

5. Fire trains put out fires in tunnels and by train tracks.

6. An airport fire vehicle is a special fire engine at an airport.

23

Index

airport fire vehicle 20, 21

equipment 4, 8, 12

fireboats 18, 19

fire engines 4, 5, 6

fire helicopters 14, 15

fire motorcycles 8, 9

fire planes 12, 13

fire trains 16, 17

fire trucks 10, 11

foam 9, 21

hose 7, 16, 21

ladder 6, 7

lights 5

panniers 8

sirens 4, 5

wildfires 10, 12

Web Sites

www.911forkids.com/

encyclopedia.kids.net.au/page/pa/Paramedic

Kidshealth.org/Kid/watch/er/911.html

BEEEEP!